JUL 1 1 2017

P9-AZV-690

SPRINGDALE PUBLIC LIBRARY
405 S. PLEASANT
SPRINGDALE, AR 72764
479-750-8180

For Mark
—L.M.

To my friend Lee Wardlaw,
for her early encouragement and mentorship
—D.R.O.

Text copyright © 2017 by Lauren McLaughlin
Jacket art and interior illustrations copyright © 2017 by Debbie Ridpath Ohi
All rights reserved. Published in the United States by Random House Children's Books,
a division of Penguin Random House LLC, New York.
Random House and the colophon are registered trademarks of Penguin Random House LLC.
Visit us on the Web! randomhousekids.com
Educators and librarians, for a variety of teaching tools, visit us at RHTeachersLibrarians.com

Library of Congress Cataloging-in-Publication Data is available upon request.

ISBN 978-0-449-81916-6 (trade) — ISBN 978-0-375-97177-8 (lib. bdg.) — ISBN 978-0-375-98161-6 (ebook)

MANUFACTURED IN CHINA
10 9 8 7 6 5 4 3 2 1
First Edition

Random House Children's Books supports the First Amendment and celebrates the right to read.

Mitzi Tulane

Preschool Detective

IN

The Secret Ingredient

by Lauren McLaughlin • illustrated by Debbie Ridpath Ohi

Random House 🏠 New York

SPRINGDALE PUBLIC LIBRARY
405 S. PLEASANT
SPRINGDALE, AR 72764
479-750-8180

Mitzi Tulane, Preschool Detective,
was playing with her friend Max.

They had already investigated
Mommy's shoe closet; spied on
Daddy, who was on the phone
with someone named "Work" . . .

 . . . and searched for evidence under Baby Kev's crib.
It was a slow day.
Until snack time rolled around.

"Don't eat that," said Max.
"Why not?" asked Mitzi. She
loved her father's muffins.

Max scooted close. "Sometimes,"
he whispered, "my mom sneaks
things into my food."
"Like what?" asked Mitzi.

Max scooted even closer.
"Like . . . spinach."
Mitzi was stunned. She knew
Max's mother, who didn't seem
like the type.

"She's always sneaking vegetables into my food," said Max. "And she thinks I can't tell. That's the worst part."

Mitzi stared at the muffin, wondering if her father could be as sneaky as Max's mom.

Then she dragged Max and the muffin into her bedroom. She inspected it with her magnifying glass. It looked like an ordinary muffin. But no good detective would leave it at that, so she broke it into a million pieces. And there, amidst the crumbly crumbs, was something so small you could hardly see it.

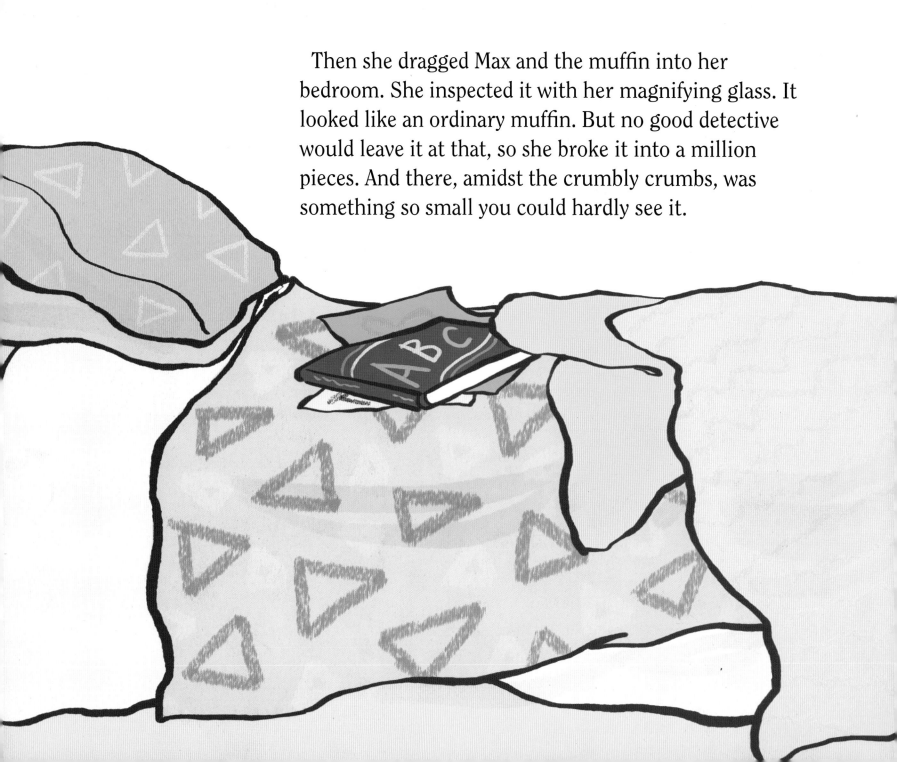

"Max," ordered Mitzi, "hand me that plastic bag. We've got work to do."

While Daddy continued his phone call with "Work," Mitzi and Max snuck out of the apartment and across the hall.

"No unnecessary noise," Mitzi whispered. "Or the super, Tall Dan, will hear us and—" But it was too late.

Tall Dan was staring at them with his mop and his bucket and that big goofy smile on his face.

"What's in the bag, buckaroos?" he asked.

"I can't disclose that information," said Mitzi. "And don't call us buckaroos."

Mitzi led Max to Apartment 6H, where the twins, Juan and Juanita, lived. They were her go-to neighbors when cases took a more technical turn.

"Step into our crime lab," said Juan.

Inside, it was a miracle of science. There were petri dishes and microscopes, probes and forceps, and all manner of investigative and pointy instruments.

Mitzi gave them the evidence. "It's so small," she explained, "you can hardly see it."

"No problem," said Juanita. "We'll see it with science."

With state-of-the-art forceps, Juanita placed the crumb
between two slides, then examined it under her microscope.
"Is it spinach?" Mitzi gulped.

"I'm afraid the evidence is inconclusive," said Juanita. "We're going to have to consult Bun Bun. He's the only one who can verify our theory."

"So you have a theory?" asked Mitzi.

"Please," said Juanita. "We mustn't rush this."

In a corner of the lab, Juan and Juanita lifted a cloth to reveal a cage filled with straw, some celery, and a water bottle with a metal spout. Juan lowered the evidence right inside the cage.

"Stand back," he warned. "Bun Bun does not like to be crowded."

Mitzi hugged Gigi Gaboo close while Max gripped her hand. A moment later . . .

. . . Bun Bun appeared from beneath a pile of straw.
He approached the evidence that was too small to see.

His nose wiggled. He
sniffed the air.

Then, all at once, he pounced on the evidence and consumed it!

SPRINGDALE PUBLIC LIBRARY
405 S. PLEASANT
SPRINGDALE, AR 72764
479-750-8180

"I knew it!" said Juanita.
"No," said Juan. "You only suspected.
Now you know."

"I stand corrected," said Juanita. "Detective Tulane, what we have here is . . .

". . . a trace of carrot."

"Uuuuugggghhh!" cried Max. "What kind of a madman puts carrots in a muffin?"

"The kind of madman I call Daddy," said Mitzi. "That's who."

"But why can't a muffin just be a muffin?" cried Max. "Does everything need to have a stinking vegetable crammed into it?"

"No, it doesn't," said Mitzi, while Juan got Max a soothing glass of milk. "But sometimes you have to deal with the world as it is, Max, not the way you'd like it to be. Isn't that right, Gigi Gaboo?"

Gigi looked back with a world-weary gaze. She'd learned *this* lesson long ago.

"Juan and Juanita," said Mitzi, "write up your results."
"Way ahead of you," said Juanita, who handed her the report.

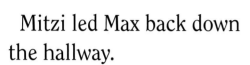

Mitzi led Max back down the hallway.

"What's on the paper?" asked Tall Dan.

"Proof," said Mitzi. "Proof that sometimes the culprit is right under your nose."

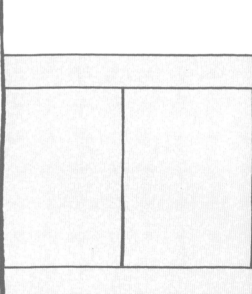

"Yeah," said Max. "And that's why the world needs a preschool detective."